ORION
THE SKATEBOARD KID

JUANITA S. RAYMOND
LELAND F. RAYMOND

[signature: Juanita Raymond]

CyPress
Publications

Tallahassee, Florida

Inquiries should be addressed to:
CyPress Publications
P.O. Box 2636
Tallahassee, Florida 32316-2636

Library of Congress Catalog Card Number: 99-091210

ISBN 0-9672585-0-2

First Edition

Dedication

For our sons, Jason and Daniel
May they know their paths by following in our footsteps.

Acknowledgments

A book is a magical thing, a physical embodiment of a dream. No dream becomes a reality without the efforts of many people. We would like to thank all those who read and listened to our story: Our sons Jason and Daniel, our nephew Jeremy and our friend Stephanie Barraco who were our first student readers. Great thoughts often come from young minds, and your suggestions were invaluable. Thank you Debra Gresko, Julia Horigan, Cynthia Johnson and Debora Page who read our early drafts and encouraged us from the beginning. Thanks to all our nieces and nephews who sat patiently and listened. Thanks to our fellow writers Carol Cordoba, Leedell Neyland, and thanks also to Barbara Hogan and the other members of the Tallahassee Writers' Association who believed in us and encouraged us to keep writing and editing and rewriting. Thanks to Adele Smith, Marvel Lou Sandon, Judy Renwick, Dorothy Inman-Crews, and Joan Cooey of the Florida State University Developmental Research School who gave us an audience of young minds; and to all the children and parents who inspired us.

Special thanks to Kathleen Carr, not only for your editorial suggestions, but also for your environmental and science expertise. Special thanks also to Della Orsini for your expertise in graphics and publication.

In memory of Aziza Bryant.

Preface

From our modern perspective, it is difficult for us to imagine the night skies of ancient peoples.

Looking out from a hillside tonight, we see the million lights of a city before us, like a blanket of jewels on an open field. In the east, stadium lights turn night into day while teams entertain their fans. To the south, a bright glow rains upward and a widening beam sweeps steadily across the horizon, marking the site of the airport for approaching aircraft. To the north, a trio of klieg lights beckon shoppers to the latest "Grand Opening Sale." And all around, cars thread their way to and from the city in flowing rivers of red and white.

Looking out from a hillside in the year 2,000 B.C., the shepherd tending his flock saw to the east the warm flickering glow of his fellow shepherds' campfires. To the south, he saw his herd, washed in the pale glow of the moon. To the north, he saw the silver, moonlit river, threading its way toward his village where the warm glow of oil lamps leaked from shuttered windows. And above all, he saw the million lights of the stars, like a blanket of jewels on an open field.

To ancient civilizations, the stars were much more than sparkling jewels illuminating the night sky. Without the distractions of modern city night life, without the effects of electric light pollution—which obscures so many stars—ancient peoples could clearly see patterns and shapes in the night sky. And surely, if there were shapes and patterns, they must have been placed there for a purpose by some powerful, supernatural being. They must have been placed there to teach the people of Earth how to live.

Throughout history, in all cultures, the stars provided inspiration for religious belief and practical guidance for everyday life. Thus, Astronomy, the scientific study of the stars, was vitally important to ancient peoples.

Astronomy is equally important to us today. Only by learning about the stars—including our own star, the Sun—can we discover scientific explanations about the evolution of stars and the universe, the processes involved in planetary formation, the origins of life on Earth, and even how to preserve life on Earth. We must, therefore, instill in our young people a desire to learn Astronomy.

Our experience in introducing young people to Astronomy, however, illustrated a problem: Young people have a great deal of difficulty recognizing the constellations, which are the basic means of locating objects in the sky. Why? Because the shapes traditionally identified as Orion the Hunter, Ursa Major and Ursa Minor (Big Bear and Little Bear), or Pegasus mean nothing to today's young people. They are unable to see Orion the Hunter because the shape looks nothing like today's hunters.

Orion the Skateboard Kid is offered as a solution to this problem. Just as ancient peoples identified shapes in the night sky that had meaning in their lives, people today can identify shapes that have meaning in their lives. When we tell young people, "Picture a kid on a skateboard doing a jump into the air, arms up for balance and knees bent," they have no problem seeing the shape of Orion in the sky; the shape is one they recognize instantly. If identifying the mythological shapes of the constellations poses a problem, simply create a new modern mythology.

In *Orion the Skateboard Kid,* Orion Hunter represents any child of any ethnic culture: Her parents, teachers, neighbors, authority figures, friends and community all play a vital role in this story because they are so important to the welfare of each child. It is, after all, society's responsibility, as well as the parents', to provide the right paths for kids to follow as they grow. Values such as safety, courtesy, and respect for family, community and country are as old as mythology and as modern as a skateboard.

Using a Star Chart

The star chart on the following page represents the view of the evening sky during most of the winter for mid-northern latitudes. It also shows the sky on a fall morning or a spring evening.

To use a star chart, remember it is made to view over your head. Turn it so the direction you are facing is at the bottom. Find a constellation you recognize, and locate others by using the stars you know as pointers. You should know the Sun rises in the east and sets in the west. You are facing north if west is to your left and east is to your right. To be sure you are facing north, look for Ursa Major and use the last two stars in the bowl to locate Polaris, the North Star, the only star located directly over our North Pole.

Star Chart Shows
Fall Mornings
Winter Nights
Spring Evenings

NORTH

EAST

WEST

URSA
MINOR

CASSIOPEIA

Polaris

Capella
and Kids

URSA
MAJOR

AURIGA

PLEIADES

GEMINI

TAURUS

Castor

ORION

Aldebaran
HYADES

Pollux

Betelgeuse

Procyon

Rigel

CANIS
MAJOR

Sirius

SOUTH

Type Style Shows
CONSTELLATION TITLES
CLUSTER TITLES
Star Titles

CHAPTER 1 ORION RISING

Orion Hunter woke up early that fall morning. It was still dark as her feet searched for her slippers on the cold tile floor. She wrapped herself in her robe, her heart pounding with excitement as she thought about starting middle school today. She bounded down the stairs and into the kitchen where Dad was making breakfast.

"You're up bright and early," Dad said as she sat at the counter by the Sunrise Window.

"It's still dark," she said. "Is it too early to get ready for school?"

"You don't have to leave for school until 7:30. You have plenty of time to eat breakfast first. Watch for the sunrise; Mom should get home from work about that time."

Orion turned around and looked out the window. She was soon lost in her own thoughts.

She watched Dad's reflection in the window as he came up behind her and put a plate of scrambled eggs, toast and a glass of milk on the counter. He smiled, pulled up his stool, and they sat side by side looking out at the dark, cool, north Florida morning.

They lived on one of the last foothills of the Appalachian Mountains, just west of Tallahassee, Florida's Capital City. They could watch the sun rise over the city from this window. That's why Orion had named this the Sunrise Window the first day they lived in the house.

"Orion, see those three stars in a row just above the pointed pine?" Dad asked as he gently took her chin and turned it up. She could see the pointed pine. That was no problem. The sun was just starting to tint the sky behind the trees, and even though the rest of the sky was black, the trees were clearly outlined along the horizon. She followed the point of the tallest pine tree up into the darkness, up to the three stars sparkling like diamonds in the sky. They seemed to dangle from the upper window pane like crystals on a string.

"Yeah, I see them!" she whispered, as if she and Dad shared a secret. The stars were beautiful, so bright, so clear. For a moment, she forgot everything else and watched the sky.

"You were named after those stars," Dad said. "Those three stars in a row are Orion's belt. The rest of those stars, from just above the Capitol Building to just before the airport," he pointed from the upper left of the window pane to the right across the dawn colors, "they make up the rest of the Orion constellation."

Orion looked up where her father pointed. The stars shone as bright as city lights on the horizon, but she could clearly see the row of three stars forming Orion's belt.

She watched the three glittering stars as she ate, while Dad told her the rest of her name story. "It didn't matter if you were a boy or a girl; you were going to be named Orion." Dad leaned toward her and continued. "The day we found out Mom was pregnant with you, she was so excited she began experimenting with names to see if she liked the sound of them.

"Since Mom works nights, she sometimes has trouble sleeping when she's off from work. One night, Mom went outside so she wouldn't disturb me, and saw three stars rise above the trees just like this," he said pointing to the pine tree and up to the stars. "She knew she recognized them, but she couldn't remember their names. Mom woke me up while searching for her old astronomy book. I came out of the bedroom just as she dropped down to the floor with that massive paperback book, scanned the index, flipped the pages and opened it. 'There it is!' she said, pointing to a photograph of stars. 'It's Orion the Hunter!' "

"Orion the Hunter," Orion repeated, nodding.

Dad stood, gave Orion a hug and started washing the breakfast dishes. Orion stared at the stars while she finished her milk. She couldn't stop thinking about her mom, her name, and school. . . . *She was going to middle school today!*

2

CHAPTER 2 SUNRISE

Mom pulled into the driveway and got out of the car, pausing for a moment to watch the brilliant dawn. There was a tiny sliver of a moon rising just above the first rays of sunshine and just below Orion the Hunter. Her Orion was going to start middle school today, she thought as she entered the house. She went into the kitchen and found Orion staring out the window.

"Good morning, young lady," Mom said and hugged Orion. "You watching the moon come up? Isn't it just beautiful?"

The sky had turned orange and pale blue through the trees. "No," Orion exclaimed as she turned, "I'm watching Orion's belt!"

"Really!" her mom said surprised.

"Right there above the trees, see?" Orion turned back to the window and pointed to the spot just above the trees, and—there was the slender crescent of the moon! She raised her finger up a couple of inches and pointed; *there* was the row of three shining stars. "They moved, Mom! The stars were above the pointed pine tree, and now the moon is!"

Orion's mom smiled. "The moon and the stars rise and set, just like the sun. Don't you remember naming this window that faces east the Sunrise Window and the window in your bedroom that faces west the Sunset Window?"

Orion nodded, "I remember."

Mom took the tiny globe key chain she always carried and explained. "Because the earth rotates once every day," she twirled the colorful blue ball counterclockwise in front of the window, "the sun seems to rise in the east over the city. It travels across the sky to straight overhead at noon, and then it sets in the west over the forest at bedtime. This is called apparent motion."

Orion looked puzzled, and her mom reassured her. "Don't worry. If it doesn't make sense now, just think about it a while, and someday you'll think you've always known. Right now, you have to get ready for school."

Orion got up from the counter and ran upstairs to her bedroom. The room was still dark, and she remembered Mom calling one of her windows the Sunset Window. Cool! But there are two windows in my room, she thought. One looks out over the forest; that's the Sunset Window. The other looks to the north out over the street; I'll have to think of a name for that window. She turned on the light, saw her supplies all laid out, and forgot about everything but school.

Orion the Hunter

Most cultures see in this constellation a great warrior, hunter or leader. In Greek Mythology, Orion the Hunter was the greatest hunter on Earth. He claimed he was so strong that he could hunt and slay the mightiest animals. To teach him a lesson for bragging, the gods sent a lowly scorpion to ambush and kill Orion. Orion's friends were so upset over his death, they begged the gods to place Orion's likeness in the sky.

Orion can be seen rising from behind the Sun in the early morning hours of late summer. Each morning, Orion seems to make one step further into the night. Throughout the fall, Orion will dominate the morning sky. Finally, by the New Year, the great hunter can be seen rising in the east as the Sun sets in the west. Note the bright blue giant star, Rigel, and the brilliant red giant star, Betelgeuse. Orion disappears in the west as the Sun sets in early spring.

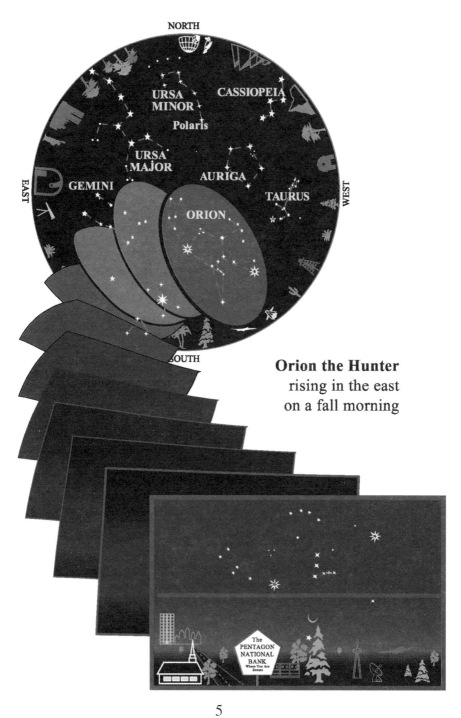

Orion the Hunter
rising in the east
on a fall morning

The
PENTAGON
NATIONAL
BANK
Where You Are
Secure

5

CHAPTER 3 SCHOOL IS COOL

Middle school was so wonderful, it never occurred to Orion that she was there to learn. Oh, she was pretty smart, especially in geography and sports, but that was because Mom and Dad had maps all over the house. And they coached her baseball team, so these things seemed to come naturally.

Mom had put a giant glow-in-the-dark star chart over her bed and a huge relief map of the world, the type you can feel the mountains on, by her bedside. In the dark, before Orion went to sleep, she would feel the Rocky Mountains where she was born and follow them down to New Mexico, then find the shoreline of the Gulf of Mexico in Texas and trace it across the Mississippi River to Florida where she lived now.

Just before Orion fell asleep, she would look up at the glowing star chart and remember Mom saying she could use the stars to find her way back to Colorado one day. All she had to do was find the bowl of the Big Dipper and connect the two stars at the end of the bowl just opposite the handle. Then, just like a dot-to-dot picture, draw a line four times their distance to the North Star.

Mom had even written this down, as if Orion might someday follow the instructions. "Find the dim but stationary star, Polaris, the only star directly over the North Pole, the sky's turning point. Keep it shining on your right shoulder until you get to New Mexico, then turn to face it and follow it until you cross into Colorado."

"Right, Mom, I got it," Orion would joke whenever Mom told her these directions. But she always thought of the North Star as her Home Star.

Dad was cool; everything he said made sense. He could talk about computer games, baseball, football, Frisbee, bicycles, soccer, even in-line skates and skateboards. And even though he was now a teacher at the elementary school, he rarely turned things into a lesson the way Mom did.

If there was any kind of game, she and Dad would play it. But of all the toys and games Orion had, her skateboard was her most prized possession. And now that she was able to walk to school without Dad, she rode her board to school every day and had mastered it.

The daily routine was great. Since Mom still worked the night shift, Orion would have breakfast before Mom got home from work; then Orion and Dad would make a big deal out of tucking Mom into bed before they took off for the day. Dad would see that Orion had everything she needed, lock up the house, then head west toward the elementary school. Orion would head east toward the middle school, making a slight detour to the garage where her skateboard lay waiting for her.

With a big skip, she would bound through the door, step on the board with her right foot and press down with her toe, popping the back of the board up to her outstretched hand. With the grace of a ballet dancer, she would twirl out the door, drop the board, step on it with her right foot and push off with the left, all in one fluid motion. Then she would fly down the driveway, letting the wind flutter her eyelashes as she sailed away.

Orion had the right turn at the end of the driveway onto the sidewalk down pat. If she stayed close to the inside corner and raised her foot just enough to lift the front wheels off the ground, she could shift her weight to the right, while turning the board with her raised foot. When Mom tried to explain balance to her, it seemed impossible to understand; yet when Orion rode her board, it all made perfect sense.

Vroom! Just like a roller coaster, she would spin around the corner of the driveway. There were no more houses on her street, only a large, fenced-in stormwater pond and the Pentagon National Bank at the end. With one good push just before the bank, she could fly off the sidewalk, down the access ramp and into the parking lot. This gave Orion an incredible amount of speed, and she could make it across the parking lot to the next corner, where she hopped off her board, flipped it up to her hands and carried it across the street to school.

Riding her skateboard to school was great! She arrived at school each day glowing with excitement at having made the whole trip with only three push-offs on the board.

CHAPTER 4 BEST FRIENDS

Her best friends, the Gemini twins Paul and Cas, saw Orion fly through the bank parking lot early one morning, and with great excitement, they decided to try it, too. There was another access ramp in front of the bank entrance, and when Orion arrived the following morning with the sun in her eyes, the twins were there waiting to surprise her. When they heard the clack, clack, clack of the skateboard on the sidewalk, they yelled her name, pushed off their skateboards and flew down the opposite ramp to meet her halfway in the empty parking lot.

As the twins approached, Orion stretched her hand out to Paul, locked fingers, and swung him around. When she let go, Orion catapulted back up the ramp she had just come down. Up into the air she flew! She pulled her knees up, reached down and turned the board completely around in midair. Landing back on the ramp, she flew down into the parking lot, where she and the twins high-fived, turned in unison and glided to the street corner. Awesome! Orion's heart pounded with excitement. The three decided to meet there after school and see if they could do their trick again.

All day Orion felt as if she were in motion every time she remembered flying up off the ramp. Her feet would tingle, and she would shiver with excitement as she anticipated a repeat performance that afternoon.

After school she ran for her locker, grabbed her board and headed for the corner. She wasn't even out of the school driveway when she saw the cars in the bank parking lot. Of course, she thought, that's why she never rode the board home. Cars! As usual the lot was full, and a few cars had parked on the grass in front of the holding pond by her house. Even the sidewalk was out of the question for this afternoon.

The twins bounded up beside her. "Ready, Orion?" Paul asked. "Let's roll!" said Cas.

Orion rolled her eyes. "Duh, look at the cars, guys!"

The twins' faces fell. The three sat by the curb on their skateboards.

"What'll we do now?" asked Paul.

"No way we can skateboard here in the afternoons," said Cas.

"Well," Orion reassured the twins, "it's still clear in the mornings."

The friends decided to meet at the bank every morning for the rest of their lives. It was a great way to start the day, and if the twins wanted to, they could come to her house after school and ride in her driveway. Orion's dad had helped her build a small ramp, and even though it wasn't as nice as the one at the bank parking lot, it would do.

The Gemini Twins

In mythology, Pollux and Castor, the Gemini Twins, were sons of a god and a mortal, Jupiter and Leda; thus, Pollux was born immortal and Castor mortal. When Castor died, as all mortals do, Pollux pleaded with Jupiter to let the brothers remain together. Jupiter placed the two as stars in the sky so they could be together forever.

Pollux and Castor stand high on Orion's shoulder star, Betelgeuse. They rise in the east just before the Sun on crisp fall mornings. During the cold winter, the twins can be seen along the ecliptic, which is the path the Sun, Moon and planets follow from east to west through the sky.

Gemini can be seen until late spring, when it sets behind the Sun in the west. To find Gemini, first find Orion, then draw an imaginary line north from Rigel through Betelgeuse up to the twin stars Pollux and Castor.

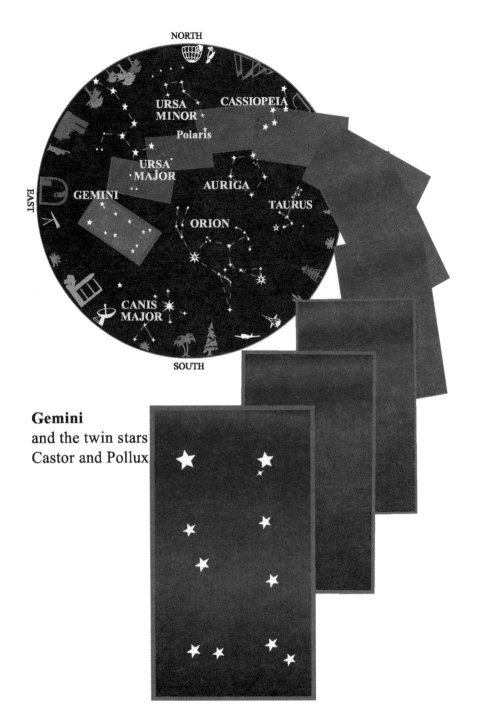

NORTH

URSA
MINOR

CASSIOPEIA

Polaris

URSA
MAJOR

AURIGA

GEMINI

TAURUS

ORION

EAST

CANIS
MAJOR

SOUTH

Gemini
and the twin stars
Castor and Pollux

CHAPTER 5 ORION SOARS ALL WINTER

Throughout the winter, Orion and the twins met early every morning to perform their quick, radical routine. By now, the twins could turn in midair just like Orion, and the bond between the three friends grew; they were inseparable. Rainy days were almost unbearable because they couldn't get together and ride their boards. Sundays were out of the question, too, because the church across the street used the bank parking lot all day long. So, every school day after her dad left for work, Orion stepped onto her board and raced out to meet her friends at the parking lot.

Spring break arrived, and Orion missed her morning routine with the twins. Dad was on break, too, and they would do something fun every day. The problem was he didn't ride a skateboard.

Dad did, however, buy Orion a cool new outfit. He called it her Orion Suit. "Puh-leeze, Dad," she said, rolling her eyes. "Don't ever say that in front of my friends!"

The outfit itself was simple. An oversized black shirt with pants to match. Mom just about had a fit when she saw the outfit; she said it was not suitable for Easter. But Orion promised to dress up the outfit with a belt and some costume jewelry. Finally, Mom gave in; and Easter Sunday, when everyone else was wearing plain old pastels, there was Orion, shining like stars in a dark sky.

The accessories made the outfit special. Orion glued three big diamond-like stones on a black belt, just like Orion the Hunter's. She sprayed glitter at each end of a long black nylon sash and arranged it evenly over her right shoulder, securing it with the big red beetle-bug pin she called Betelgeuse, and fastening it again under the belt.

The sash hung down to her knees and was so wide that it would float around her waist when Orion turned, just like the ice dancers' costumes in the Olympics. She got a floppy hat and attached the brim to the front of the hat with three crystal star-shaped buttons.

The final touch to the outfit was a pair of running shoes that flashed whenever Orion walked. Mom had found shoes that made super blue sparks at the heel. "Rigel, the star at the foot of Orion the Hunter, is a blue giant," she said. Orion was becoming a pro at rolling her eyes at Mom's corny comments, but as long as Dad was the only one around to hear, it was no problem.

CHAPTER 6 RESPECT AND THE LAW

Orion couldn't wait to go back to school after spring break. She wore her new outfit, and just as she expected, when she rode her skateboard the rhinestones sparkled in the morning sunshine, and the sash flowed behind her in the wind. Orion was watching rainbows, reflected on the sidewalk by the crystals on her hat, when she heard the familiar "Orion!". Instinctively, she stepped down and pushed off the board. Orion flew toward the ramp and was in mid-turn when she caught something moving out of the corner of her eye.

Sirius, the twins' big golden retriever, was running toward her, heading right into her path. Orion leaned to make a left turn at the end of the ramp, but as she did, another object came into view.

Before she could think, a gleaming silver van flashed through the parking lot. Time seemed to stop as she saw the horrified frozen faces of the twins and the driver of the van. The startled driver seemed to have sucked his chin into his neck, and the twins looked like stick figures drawn in the air—all outstretched arms and legs, eyes bulging in surprise.

The van seemed to pass by in slow motion. Orion jammed her back foot down. She felt the board scrape the ramp as she turned her front foot to the left. As she cleared the end of the ramp, her board turned out of harm's way. But the speed at which she was going, combined with the drag of the back end, sent her flying off the board. She took two steps and halted with the grace of a gymnast.

The danger had passed. The driver stopped the van and ran over. "Are you alright?" he asked breathlessly. They stood there staring at each other in shock; then he muttered something Orion couldn't understand, ran back to the van and drove off. Sirius barked a final reproach at the van and ran back to lick the twins' faces.

"You guys okay?" Orion finally asked with a shaky voice.

14

"Yeah, you okay, Orion?" Paul repeated.

"A bit shook up, but I'm fine," she answered. "What about your boards?" The boys spun around and saw them near Orion's. The boards must have shot under the van when they jumped off! They sat down on the curb to catch their breath. Another car came from around the back of the building.

"What gives!" Cas exclaimed as the three friends jumped up and ran to the end of the building. They were careful to stay on the sidewalk now, and as they peered around the bank, they saw it. A new drive-through automatic teller. It apparently had been installed during spring break. No warning, no signs saying "Coming Soon." And no more empty parking lot.

"Aw, man!" Cas complained as the three dropped down to the sidewalk to pout. It didn't have to be said out loud; they couldn't skateboard here before school any more and they knew it.

They sat in silence for a moment, and when the school bell rang the first warning, Orion jumped to her feet. "Go on home, Sirius. We're okay, and you shouldn't be out loose like this." She leaned down and gave the faithful dog a warm hug. "Thanks for the warning, Sirius; you're a real hero." She stood up, took a deep breath and looked at the twins. "We better get going or we'll be late."

Paul started to stand, but Cas held him down. "No way, Orion," he said. "We're not going to school. That guy almost ran us over. We're going home."

"NO YOU'RE NOT!" a deep gravelly voice bellowed from behind them. The children's heads spun around, and they looked over and up to the biggest authority figure they had ever seen. Major Ursa, the new sheriff, was glaring down at them, a bear of a man with massive fists tucked into his sides.

Orion had seen his picture on election posters last fall when the school kids had voted, but she never imagined how big he would be in person.

15

Major Ursa looked like the ultimate law enforcer. Orion, who was the biggest kid in her class, stood only to his elbow. When he took his fist off his hip, Orion thought it resembled a football.

The sheriff pointed his finger down close to the twins' faces and with each poke barked out orders:

"YOU'LL not only GO to school, but you'll also READ, in front of the WHOLE CLASS, Town Code Sections 12-98 and 12-99 which PERTAIN to OBSTRUCTING TRAFFIC and wearing PROTECTIVE EQUIPMENT while riding bicycles, SKATEBOARDS and in-line skates."

Major Ursa turned to Orion now and, with the same pronounced gestures, said, "And YOU will read Town Code Section 12-100, which prohibits SKATEBOARDS and in-line skates on SIDEWALKS and in PARKING lots."

Paul crossed his arms on his chest and complained, "Aw, man!" while he shifted his weight from one foot to the other. His eyes rolled, and he gave Major Ursa his most defiant look.

Cas argued and dared to stamp his foot. He pointed in the direction the van had gone. "That driver almost ran us over and we're in trouble?"

"Sergeant Little Bear," Major Ursa bellowed, so loud that the boys immediately shut up. "Confiscate these skateboards and escort these delinquents to the school. I am going to pay a visit to their parents and principal."

Reluctantly, the kids gave up their precious boards, and with sinking hearts, they marched off to school. The thought of Major Ursa waking her mom from her first hour of sleep sent waves of nausea through Orion. Mom would be disoriented and would panic when she saw the big sheriff at the door. Orion ran back to Major Ursa.

"Major Ursa, my mother works nights and she just got to bed. She'll panic if she wakes up to the doorbell and sees you blocking the entrance. Could you tell my dad instead?" She gave him directions, and Major Ursa touched the brim of his big Smoky Bear hat and said he would speak to her dad.

Auriga the Charioteer

Auriga is made up of five major stars which form a pentagon shape. In mythology, Auriga rides his chariot with three baby goats under his arm. Some cultures see Auriga as a spider web, and others see it as the shell on the turtle's back.

Auriga rises in the northeast before sunrise in mid-summer. By the time school begins and throughout the cold winter, the pentagon shape seems to fill the Zenith (the top of the sky) between Orion and Cassiopeia. To find Auriga, imagine that the V-shaped face of Taurus has giant horns which extend north, and the right horn shares the bottom left star in Auriga.

Look to the upper right of Auriga and find Capella, the brightest star in the pentagon. The small triangle of stars below Capella is called The Kids.

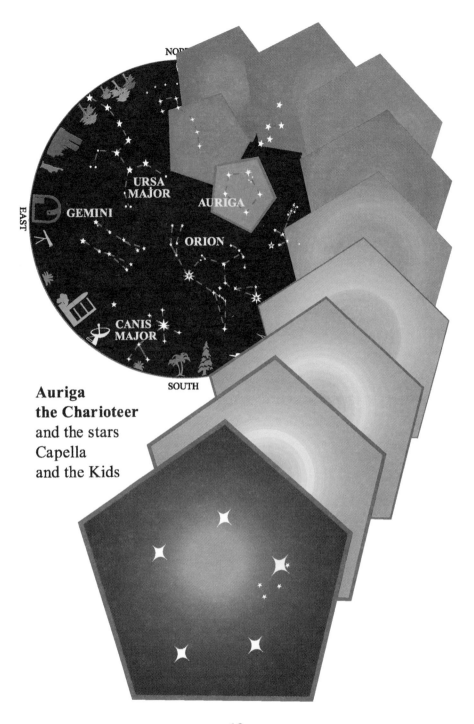

**Auriga
the Charioteer**
and the stars
Capella
and the Kids

19

CHAPTER 7 EARTH TO ORION

They sat outside the principal's office during the whole first period. "We're missing Physical Education," Paul grumbled, "our favorite class."

"Yeah," Cas added, "but we won't miss Science, that's for sure."

Shortly after second period began, the principal handed them their Town Code sections and sent them to class. Orion resented being late. Now she had to interrupt Ms. Cassio's science lesson, admit she was in trouble and then read the Town Code section as punishment. With her head down, Orion opened the science teacher's door and made for her desk.

Since Ms. Cassio used a wheelchair, the desks were set up in a semicircle around the simple podium she used for her notes. Orion's desk was not far from the door, and Ms. Cassio did not mention her tardiness as she took her seat.

Peggy, one of her classmates, was speaking, but Orion didn't understand what she was saying. When Peggy finished, Ms. Cassio said, "Thank you for your presentation on fire extinguishers. So, now we know that proper ventilation, exercising caution, reading instructions and knowing how to use a fire extinguisher are all very important lab safety rules. Any other safety tips we should discuss?"

Several other students raised their hands, and in turn, Ms. Cassio went around the class collecting valuable tips on lab safety, such as wearing safety glasses, and washing your hands and equipment after completing an experiment. Orion tried to take notes and listen, but she knew she would soon be called upon and humiliated as she told her classmates what she had done.

Ms. Cassio's soothing voice continued toward the end of the hour. "Safety is important outside the classroom as well. Archie, read the school's policy on using the crosswalks and obeying the crossing guard." She handed him the small Middle School Handbook they had all been given at the first of the year, and Archie read on.

The minutes passed, and the students discussed having spotters in Physical Education, swimming using the buddy system, and finally, safety when traveling.

"Whether you are wearing a seat belt while riding in a car or looking both ways before you cross a street, you must think about safety," said Ms. Cassio. "Sometimes, you are not told things are dangerous or against the law, such as riding your bicycle on a sidewalk. But that doesn't automatically mean that it is legal or safe. Cas, read Town Code Section 12-98 about obstructing traffic."

Cas stood and glanced at Orion and Paul before reading the single paragraph.

> No person upon roller skates or riding in or upon or by means of any coaster, skateboard, toy vehicle or similar device shall go upon any roadway, except while crossing a street or crosswalk, and when so crossing, such person shall be granted all of the rights and shall be subject to all of the duties applicable to pedestrians. This section shall not apply upon any street which has been set aside as a play street under authority of the town traffic engineer.

When Cas was finished, the class discussed bicycles and the rules of the road. Paul was next, and he read Town Code Section 12-99 on required safety gear.

> Any person under 16 years of age, while riding upon bicycles, skateboards, roller skates or by means of any type of toy vehicle or similar device, shall wear protective headgear within the town limits.

There was a brief discussion on whether or not the Code was fair. Finally, Ms. Cassio turned to Orion and said, "Please read Town Code Section 12-100."

Orion stood and bravely read the paragraphs loud and clear; she had no intention of having to repeat this punishment.

Prohibitions. Skateboards and in-line skates are prohibited on all streets, sidewalks, alleys and parking areas within the downtown business district.

Skateboard means a board made of wood, fiberglass, plastic, metal or other material or combination of materials mounted on two or more axles, front and rear, with two or more wheels made of clay, polyurethane, rubber or other material or combination of materials attached to each axle. The word "skateboard" includes motorized skateboards propelled by a motor mounted on the skateboard.

As soon as Orion finished, before she had the chance to sit in her seat, the bell rang. She stood, numb with anxiety over the morning's events.

Orion became aware that someone was speaking to her, and turned to see Peggy waving her arms. "Earth to Orion! Earth to Orion! I said nice outfit, Orion. Wake up!"

Orion smiled and looked down at her sash. "Thanks, Peggy," she said. Orion scooped up her books and began to walk toward the door.

Suddenly, she turned and glanced at Ms. Cassio. Their eyes met, and Orion realized that the teacher had given her the chance to fulfill her punishment without being humiliated. Ms. Cassio must have understood how her classmates would have teased her if they had known.

Orion nodded toward her teacher with the same respect one would pay to a queen, and Ms. Cassio nodded in return.

CHAPTER 8 ORION AT SUNSET

Mom and Dad were so upset by the time Orion got home that afternoon that they had prepared a speech. Mom said that, for now, Orion should just listen to what they had to say and tomorrow, when they could speak more calmly, they would let her explain. Dad said, "I had no idea you were returning to the house each day to get your skateboard. If I had known, I would have told you how dangerous it was to ride through town."

Mom blamed herself for not spending enough time with Orion when she came home from work. Dad blamed himself for assuming she was mature enough to make it two blocks to school each day. Now he would have to leave at least 15 minutes earlier to see that she got to school without "dilly-dallying."

Major Ursa had not spared Mom and Dad the particulars of Orion's "close encounter" and had described the incident in graphic detail. As a result, her parents were horrified to say the least, and it would be at least tomorrow before they could speak to her calmly.

They closed their speech with the instructions for the evening: Orion was to take a sandwich and a glass of water to her room; she was to keep her door open; she could not listen to her stereo; if she wished to read or write, she was to sit at her desk; she could sit on the edge of her bed if she wanted to think about what she had done that day, but no lying down until bedtime.

Orion knew she was in *very* big trouble. She went to her room and did her homework first. She tried to read a book, but she just couldn't get into the story. Her own troubles were all she could think about. Around seven o'clock, she nibbled at her meager rations, then sat down on the end of her bed.

It was early spring, and daylight savings time had started last week, so it was still light out. Orion knew the kids in the neighborhood were

23

still out playing. She could hear their shouts in the school yard, and she wondered how long it would be before she could go out and play again. As she stared out the window, the sun turned into a big orange ball on the western horizon.

A whippoorwill whistled off in the forest, and she heard a chorus of tree frogs. Orion drew in the peaceful effects of the sunset. It felt as if all the negative events of the day flowed out of her body and disappeared on the breeze. She stood and, for the first time that day, stopped thinking about her skateboard.

The sun was gone now behind the dark outline of the trees, but the horizon glowed like embers in a campfire. Orion was mesmerized. She took a breath so deep it was as if her whole body inflated and then, just as completely, deflated.

The fluorescent orange of the sunset faded, and the sky began to grow dark. Orion noticed that the whippoorwill and tree frogs were the only sounds now. She could no longer hear the children playing. They must be inside their houses for the evening.

By now the sky was totally black. There was no moon, and there were no city lights over the western forest; the darkness and chill made Orion shiver. Then out of the dark a meteor streaked across the sky. Orion gasped as the streak of light glittered, faded, and disappeared into the darkness, leaving behind a shimmering, translucent path with three diamond-like stars behind.

She stared at the spot in awe as she recognized Orion's belt. She stared for a long time at the beautiful stars that were her namesake.

Orion focused on the three gleaming stars for so long they seemed to burn themselves into her eyes and she blinked. Her eyes were so dry they seemed to scrape when she closed them. When she opened them, she saw an illustration in the sky—as if someone had just opened a giant picture book.

There was Orion the Hunter. She knew every star; she had heard Mom describe them so many times. Betelgeuse, the red giant star on Orion's right shoulder and bright blue Rigel at the left foot. The line of three identical stars at the belt with the elusive but visible sword below.

Sword! Orion thought. That's not a sword, it's my sash! Her heart thumped and then seemed to skip a beat as the day's events flooded into her thoughts.

The picture she saw before her eyes now was not Orion the Hunter, it was Orion the Skateboard Kid. Her stomach tightened as she thought about flying down that access ramp so close to the van she could see the whites of the driver's eyes.

The stars above were poised in the same stance she must have had when she tried to avoid the van. Stooped in just the right position, knees bent, chin down, arms high over her head, riding her skateboard.

Orion moved closer to the window until the screen touched her eyebrows and continued to watch the sky and think of the day. Her head reeled with the visions of what could have happened. And there in the sky before her, she could see the whole scene framed in the window pane. Like an illustration in a picture book, there was Orion tearing down the ramp, and the path of the meteor was the speeding van.

"Oh, cool!" she whispered, as she noticed the constellation Gemini just above Orion. The two starry stick figures side by side were her friends, Paul and Cas, jumping into the air to avoid the van. She studied the sky and seemed to find something to represent the entire episode. Setting quickly on the horizon, as if Orion's belt pointed right at it, was Taurus the Bull. And there on its back were the Pleiades, the cluster of six stars just like the ones on the logo of the car in the bank parking lot. She followed the stars in Orion's belt up, up, to what was

25

actually the brightest star in the sky, Sirius, in the constellation Canis Major, the big dog. If the twins' dog Sirius hadn't warned her that the van was coming, she may not have gotten out of harm's way.

Orion scanned the sky to the north above Taurus to the five stars which form Auriga the Charioteer and pictured the "Pentagon National Bank, Where You're Secure" sign. Phooey! she thought as she turned from the window and from the day's events. *Some security.*

Orion Throughout the Year

Orion dips behind the Sun quickly in the west on early spring evenings as the Earth moves toward its summer position.

During the summer, Orion cannot be seen because the Earth's position puts Orion behind the Sun at that time of year.

In the early fall, you can see Orion as it rises before the Sun while you are waiting for school to begin.

Orion dominates the entire winter night sky by rising in the east at sunset and setting in the west at sunrise.

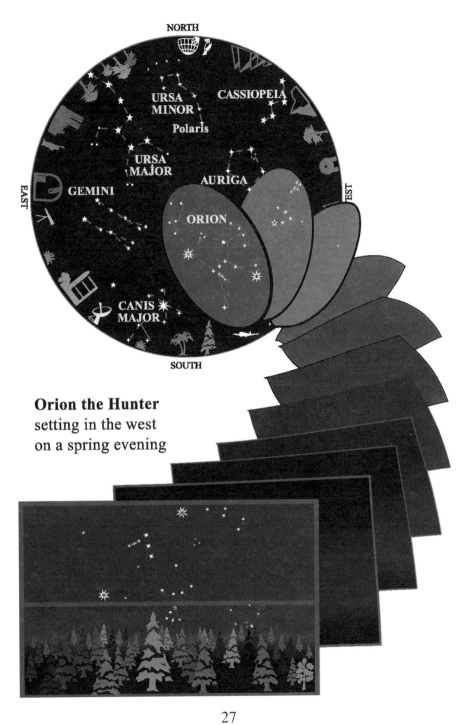

NORTH

CASSIOPEIA

URSA
MINOR

Polaris

URSA
MAJOR

AURIGA

EAST

WEST

GEMINI

ORION

CANIS
MAJOR

SOUTH

Orion the Hunter
setting in the west
on a spring evening

27

CHAPTER 9 TURNING POINT

Through her open door, Orion heard the theme music of her favorite TV show. If she planned her trip to the bathroom at just the right time, she thought she might catch a quick glimpse. Her parents must have known she would try this, because they changed the channel before the theme music ended, even though the three of them usually watched the show together.

Orion got ready for bed and said goodnight to her parents like a robot, allowing her body to take the lead while she concentrated on putting the day behind her.

In moments, she was sitting on the edge of her bed, trying to find something, anything, to be thankful for in the day's events. But the stars outside the other window in her room drew her attention; there were so many she hadn't noticed before. She walked over to the northern window, and as if someone had turned the page in her book, she saw a new illustration.

Rising high to the right of the window pane was Ursa Major. Just as in Mom's directions for returning to Colorado, Orion drew a line through the two stars at the end of the bowl of Ursa Major, four times their distance, and came to the North Star, Polaris, the sky's turning point. She remembered, now, naming this the Home Star Window because she could always see the North Star through it.

Continuing directly across Polaris, she found M-shaped Cassiopeia, Queen of ancient Ethiopia, sitting on her throne, regal and proud. She thought of her science teacher Ms. Cassio.

Orion's eyes scanned the sky over the dim North Star back to Ursa Major. The Big Dipper, as it is sometimes called, dominated the rest of the sky's features. Orion's eyes widened as she once again saw Major Ursa's giant finger pointed at her, drilling his words into her memory.

Her eyes darted back to Cassiopeia, and Orion gave a sigh of gratitude as she recalled how Ms. Cassio carried out the assigned punishment without humiliating her.

Her eyes on the stars, Orion thought of the lessons she had learned that day, and came to an important realization: For all the rules and laws and punishments out there, with everything and everyone telling her what was wrong, she still had nowhere she could safely ride her skateboard.

Nowhere at all.

"All the safety lessons, speeches and equipment on earth might keep me safe," she said to the empty room, "but what good is safe if I'm still left with nowhere to ride?" Orion's heart felt like a rock in her chest. She laid her head in her arms on the window sill and cried herself to sleep.

CHAPTER 10 THE PATH OF SHINING STARS

When Orion awoke, her arms felt frozen to her tear-stained face. She didn't know how long she had been asleep at the window, but she knew it was late because she could hear the audience whooping it up for the host on a late night show. She wiped her eyes and looked back out the window.

The Big Dipper was way up at the top of the sky now, and Cassiopeia had set. All the porch lights and driveway lights were out for the night, and the only light left in the neighborhood was the dim glow of the streetlight down the block at the bank. She moved her eyes back up to the Big Dipper looming high in the sky. Tipped upside down in that position in the sky, a dipper would have to be empty. Empty, that's how I feel, she thought, as she remembered that now there was nowhere she could ride her skateboard.

Orion noticed the reflection of some headlights in the trees across the street as a car pulled out from the bank. An automatic teller meant the bank would be in use 24 hours a day. She and the twins had planned to learn more skateboard acrobatics, but now their plans were squashed.

Orion lifted her eyes back to the stars and saw a bright band across the sky. She thought it was another reflection of more headlights, but the band stayed stationary for too long. She sighed as she realized the rich glow must be the center of the Milky Way, the stars of her own galaxy, shining like a path across the sky.

Orion had done a lot of sighing today, hadn't she? Definitely one of those days. She almost chuckled at the thought. She pushed her head against the screen and tried to look up as high as the glittering path, but the Milky Way continued beyond the window to above the house. She decided she had better not push any harder because she might push out the screen and get into even more trouble.

As she sat back and watched the magnificent path rise higher into the sky, she realized, *that's* what we need, a *path!* How can everyone go around imposing the laws, insisting kids do things safely without providing someplace they could ride safely? With a determined look on her face, she sat on the edge of her bed and planned *her* path.

CHAPTER *11* PLANNING A PATH

Morning dawned, and though Orion was ready to face the day, she put on her most pathetic look. With swollen eyes and uncombed hair, she humbly and respectfully faced her parents. She could now see more concern than anger on her mom's face and knew that the lecture and parental sentence would be less severe than she had expected. How grateful she was that she had not faced them defiantly.

Mom and Dad told her that, in order to get her skateboard back, she had to bring Major Ursa the copy of the Town Code section she had read, signed by Ms. Cassio, to prove she had fulfilled her punishment.

The rest of her punishment were routine grounding procedures all rolled into one: no TV, extra chores, restricted to the yard and, of course, curfews.

The hard part was over, and Orion had to smile. It was time to work toward making her idea a reality. She met Paul and Cas at the bank, and they all glared at the new automatic teller before crossing the street. They went straight to Ms. Cassio's classroom and waited for her to arrive. When she entered, they stood and waited for her to speak.

"Sit down," she said and rolled her chair before them. "I thought I'd wait to sign your papers until you had a chance to think. Well, did you do any thinking?" The teacher looked over her glasses and raised her eyebrows. Orion was trying to concentrate, but the eyebrows made the *M* shape similar to the constellation Cassiopeia. She was tired; her mind was obviously wandering.

She concentrated even harder. Ms. Cassio must have noticed Orion's focused look because she called on her to speak first.

"Ms. Cassio, I was looking out my window at the stars and constellations last night, and I was thinking very hard about our trouble.

Then I noticed the Milky Way, glowing like a path across the sky. Suddenly, I knew what we needed." Orion paused for a moment, cleared her throat and went on. "All the laws and safety equipment in the universe don't solve our problem if we still have nowhere safe to ride. We need a Milky Way Trail, our own path in town, where we can ride out of the way of motorized vehicles." She could hardly believe the words were her own.

Ms. Cassio nodded her head in admiration. "I couldn't agree with you more. I participate in 5K races on weekends, and I try to get in as much training as possible to stay in shape. I would love to be able to get up a little speed on these wheels of mine, but before I manage anything more than a snail's pace, I come to an intersection and have to stop."

They decided the idea should be posed to Major Ursa later that afternoon. Ms. Cassio gave them the necessary signatures and told them to keep her informed.

After school, Orion and the twins went directly to the Sheriff's Department, careful to obey every law they knew, lest they should have to face even more charges against them. Major Ursa wasn't in, and they had to wait at least 15 minutes for him to return.

While they waited, they talked about how awesome it would be to have a bike trail in town and how they would have to make sure they got a ramp or two for their skateboards. If they were wearing the proper safety equipment—gloves, elbow and knee pads, and helmets—a ramp would be cool.

Orion, Paul and Cas froze when they heard the thunderous voice of Major Ursa as he entered the building. There was an office between the entrance and where they sat, yet the sheriff sounded as if he were standing right in front of them.

Major Ursa was so tall, he seemed to cross the inner office in just two steps, and there he was, towering over them. They stood at attention as he walked to his desk and sat down.

"Good afternoon. Have you kids brought your papers?" He spoke in a cool, clear, crisp manner, like the actors on the PBS channel, and Orion felt instantly calmer.

"Yes, sir," they said all at once.

"Good," he said. "Sit down."

Very quickly, without taking their eyes off the sheriff, they put the signed Town Code pages on the desk in front of him and sat back down. "Have you anything to say for yourselves?" Major Ursa asked as he leaned back in his chair, waiting for a response.

Orion felt Paul and Cas turn to look at her as she watched the sheriff cross his massive arms on his giant chest. She gulped, and with all the courage she could muster, she repeated the idea she had suggested to Ms. Cassio, ending with, "We need our own Milky Way Trail." She didn't feel as confident as she had with Ms. Cassio, but somehow she managed to get the words out. She knew that was all that was important.

"Yeah," added Paul, "and Ms. Cassio needs a place where she can train for her races."

Major Ursa turned to Paul and asked, "*Who* is Ms. *Cassio?*"

"She's our science teacher," he replied. "We read our Town Codes in her class. She uses this really cool wheelchair that can go fast because she's into racing, but she has nowhere she can go fast safely."

Major Ursa tapped his fingers on his desk as he contemplated what they had said. Cas shifted in his seat, knowing he would be called on next. Presently, Major Ursa looked at Cas and asked, "How long have you lived in this county?"

That was an easy one. Cas sat up straight and said, "Just two years, sir."

"Well, I've lived in this county all my life. I only moved in to town when I was elected sheriff. I suppose I like riding my bike as much as you like riding your skateboards. When I lived outside the town limits, there were lots of country roads where I could ride, but when I moved here, I had to find safe places away from all the traffic." He leaned over the desk and spoke to them confidentially.

"I found an old railroad bed which runs along the perimeter of the state forest. The rails were removed from it so many years ago that you can hardly tell what it used to be. I contacted the state land use office; they told me that, if the town provided funding for a park, the state would transfer ownership."

Sparks of dreams made the twins and Orion glance quickly at each other.

Major Ursa went on: "Since the town already owns all the land adjacent to the state forest, there's a good chance that, if a group of interested citizens went before the town council, they could convince the council to convert the old railroad bed into a trail. There are already paved areas where old buildings used to stand that could be used for a skate park. Would you kids and your . . . ."

"Yes!" Orion almost shouted.

"Yeah!" said Paul. "We're with you!"

"Count us in!" said Cas.

". . . friends like to help?" Major Ursa finished, smiling broadly.

35

The Circumpolar Constellations

The constellations that are found directly over the North Pole—Ursa Major, Ursa Minor, and Cassiopeia—are known as the circumpolar constellations, since they rotate around the North Pole. Because of their location directly over the Earth's Arctic Circle, they can be seen all night from most areas in northern latitudes. Polaris, the North Star, is located almost directly over the North Pole, so it seems to be the only star that stays stationary all night while the Earth rotates.

Cassiopeia, the Queen of Ethiopia

Cassiopeia was the most beautiful woman on Earth during her reign as queen of ancient Ethiopia. She is represented as the "W" or "M" shaped constellation, where she rules from her throne throughout the night. Some Native Americans saw Cassiopeia as First Woman and Ursa Major as First Man, who dance all night around Polaris, the Home Fire of the North, to show warriors the way home.

Ursa Major
and
Ursa Minor

One of the easiest to identify constellations in the night sky is Ursa Major, the Great Bear. To people today, it more closely resembles a Big Dipper, which is just a part of the great constellation. The Big Dipper, however, helps us to find the way north by pointing out the North Star, Polaris, the only star located directly over our North Pole. Unlike the Big Dipper, the Little Dipper, as Ursa Minor is also called, does not resemble such an easily identifiable dipper shape. Its stars are not bright, and the dipper handle turns up, so it is more like a ladle pouring into the Big Dipper.

To escaping slaves prior to the Civil War, the Big Dipper resembled a drinking gourd, and they used it to point the way north to freedom. "Follow the Drinking Gourd" was a song they sang to help them remember dangers they'd face along the way.

Polaris is very important because of its location directly over the Earth's North Pole. It is like the axle on a wheel, the only star that stays stationary while the other stars turn in the sky throughout the night. Remember, it's the Earth's daily rotation that makes the stars, planets, Moon and Sun seem to rise and set. And it's the Earth's orbit around the Sun that changes our view of the stars each season.

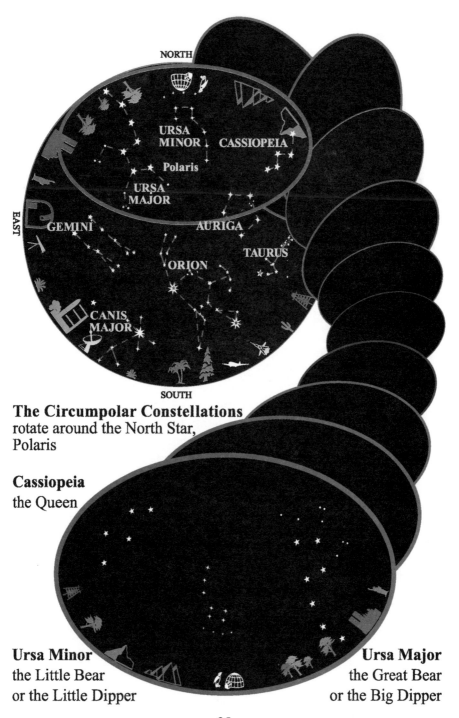

The Circumpolar Constellations
rotate around the North Star,
Polaris

Cassiopeia
the Queen

Ursa Minor
the Little Bear
or the Little Dipper

Ursa Major
the Great Bear
or the Big Dipper

38

CHAPTER *12* SUMMER SOLSTICE

Orion's dreams were only that. She had no idea how much work her project would involve.

First, Orion and her friends formed a group called The Milky Way Trail Club. The club met after school every day to prepare a speech, maps of the area and their own drawings of the skate park they hoped to build. And they went with Major Ursa to explore the area around the old railroad station.

The foundation was strewn with bricks and overgrown with brush. But the old passenger platform and the ramps once used to load and unload trade goods were still in good condition, the cement surfaces smooth and unscarred by time. Their excitement grew, and they set to work clearing the debris and preparing the site with more eagerness than they would have thought possible.

Adults were always there to help, and Orion noticed they seemed as excited about a new park in their town as the kids were. "Dad?" she asked, "do adults need a safe place to play, too?"

"When we grew up here, there was hardly any traffic to worry about," Dad explained. "We could play in the streets. Then the capital's growth began crowding our town, and we needed parks to play in. Even though we're adults now, we still appreciate our parks."

After many weeks of after-school meetings, the Milky Way Trail Club felt certain that they could convince the town council to approve their plan. Peggy stood and said, "Orion, since this was your idea, I move that we nominate you to read our presentation to the town council. Any seconds to this motion?"

"I second!" yelled both Paul and Cas. They raised their hands with such enthusiasm they almost fell out of their chairs. Peggy pounded the railroad spike they used as a gavel and said, "Orion has been nominated to be our representative at the town council meeting. All those in favor say Aye."

"Aye!" they all cheered.

"Any opposed?"

Silence.

"Orion, do you accept this responsibility?"

"I do," she said with a triumphant smile. She was still smiling when she crawled into bed that night.

The next month, the Milky Way Trail Club went to the town council meeting to present their plan. Orion, now more confident because of Ms. Cassio's and Major Ursa's encouragement, was able to present their plan quite professionally.

"Members of the Council," she began, "we are in a unique position to offer our community an opportunity not available in most areas, a safe place to ride bicycles and a park reserved for skateboard use. The location of the old North-South Railroad bed on the border of our town and the state forest gives us the chance to acquire it for public use."

Orion went to the map Major Ursa had pinned to the bulletin board and pointed out the six-mile branch of the railroad and the location of the old station platform. She handed the council members photographs of the platform and loading ramps, followed by the drawings they had prepared of what the area could be.

"Council members," she concluded, "we are here to propose a multi-use recreation area to be set aside for non-motorized vehicle and pedestrian use, complete with a park for skateboards, roller skates and in-line skates."

Mayor North thanked Orion for her presentation, and she commended the Milky Way Trail Club for all the work they had done. The children congratulated themselves with high-fives.

The council briefly discussed the proposal and decided that, before funding could be approved, they would need to know that a majority of the people in town would support such a park. A petition signed by at least 1,000 registered voters would have to be submitted along with a funding estimate.

"Man!" Cas complained, as they left the council meeting, "all the work we did was for nothing!"

41

"Yeah," added Paul, "they completely blew us off, Orion."

Orion was tempted to agree with them. Despite all the planning and preparing they had done, they still didn't have approval for their skate park, much less the Milky Way Trail itself. But she wasn't ready to give up yet.

"All the work wasn't for nothing, Cas," Orion pointed out. "They didn't *dis*approve our proposal. And they didn't blow us off, either, Paul. Maybe you were concentrating so hard on what still needs to be done that you didn't hear the mayor actually commending us for our work." The twins didn't look convinced. "We just have to get the signatures and figure out how much it'll cost. We can do it. It's a good idea, and they'll just have to approve it."

"But how are we going to get 1,000 signatures, Orion?" Peggy asked. "And where?"

Orion thought for a minute as they walked. "It's easy," she said, finally. "We'll have the people come to us!"

Taurus, the Bull

In mythology, Jupiter changed himself into many different animals for his dealings with mortals. Taurus the Bull was the shape he took to meet Europa.

Taurus rises before Orion in mid-summer. By the time school begins in the fall, it can be seen in the east high above the trees at sunrise. During the cold winter, Taurus can be seen overhead along the ecliptic. To find Taurus, use the belt of Orion and draw an imaginary arrow north (or to the right) and you come to the Great Bull.

Taurus is made up of two clusters of stars, called Hyades and Pleiades. Hyades is the V-shaped face of the Bull, with its red-eye star named Aldebaran. Pleiades is the small pan-shaped cluster to the right of Hyades. Pleiades is known in different cultures as the Seven Sisters, the Seven Little Indian Boys, and Subaru. Look at this cluster through a pair of binoculars, and you'll see why this small group of stars has so many stories to tell.

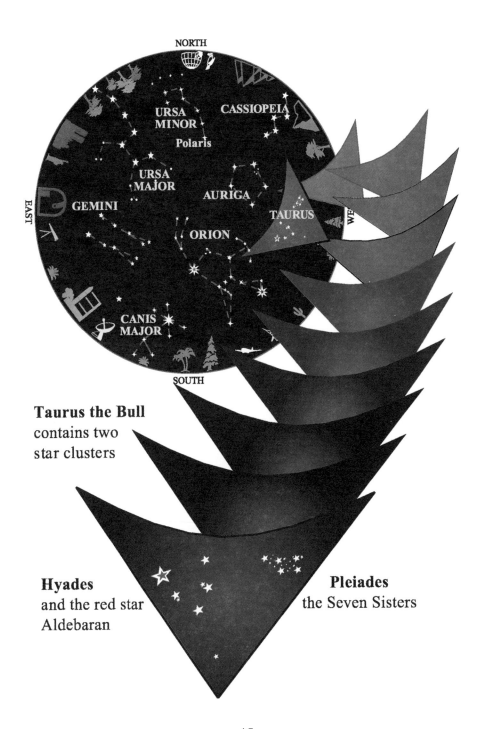

Taurus the Bull
contains two
star clusters

Hyades
and the red star
Aldebaran

Pleiades
the Seven Sisters

45

CHAPTER *14* PLANS IN MOTION

The last day of the school year had finally arrived. Paul and Cas caught up to Orion as she was leaving school.

"Yo, Orion!" Paul said. "How does it feel to be free for the whole summer?"

Orion gave the twins the customary high-fives and considered how she felt.

"I feel kinda weird," she said. "Like I'm happy and sad at the same time."

"I'm just happy," Cas said without hesitation. " 'No more school, no more books, no more teachers' dirty looks,' " he sang.

Orion laughed. "That's true, too, but I'm going to miss my teachers and all my friends. At least with no homework to do, I'll have more time to work on The Milky Way Trail plans."

"Orion, is that *all* you think about?" Paul asked.

The three friends were passing the bank parking lot, and as usual, they glared at the automatic teller machine.

"Seems like it is all I think about these days," Orion said, "but there's so much to do before the next council meeting that . . . Hey! I've got an idea. Come on!"

Orion had bounded off toward the bank entrance. The twins looked at each other, shrugged their shoulders and followed Orion through the glass door. Inside, Orion was already planted in front of the receptionist's desk.

"Mr. Megrez," Orion said, reading his nameplate, "I'd like to see the bank president, please."

A small smile played at the corner of his mouth. "Mr. Capella is with a customer right now," the receptionist said, glancing toward an office. Through the open Venetian blinds, Orion could see two men sitting on opposite sides of an ornate desk. "Would you like to wait?

It shouldn't be more than a few minutes. May I tell him the nature of your business?"

Orion took a deep breath and was about to launch into a rapid-fire explanation of The Milky Way Trail and automatic teller machines and skateboarding safely and petitions for the town council meeting when Mr. Capella emerged from his office, shaking the customer's hand as he escorted him to the door.

"Mr. Capella?" the receptionist called as the bank president turned to go back to his office. "These young people would like to see you."

"Certainly. Come right this way," the bank president said, smiling broadly. Orion, Paul and Cas trooped single-file into the office and waited nervously as Mr. Capella walked around the desk and sat down.

"Have a seat, please," he said. "What can I do for you today?"

Orion's heart was pounding in her chest. She couldn't believe she had just barged into the bank president's office on an impulse. But as long as she was here, Orion figured she might as well make the most of it. She took a deep breath to steady herself and began the long story of The Milky Way Trail. At last, her mouth dry and her knees shaking, Orion finished: "And we thought—I thought," she corrected herself, smiling at the twins, "that you, being a bank president, must know lots of important people in town. If anyone could get our Milky Way Trail built, you could. Would you help us?"

Mr. Capella had been leaning back in his chair nodding attentively, his fingers intertwined on his stomach as Orion spoke. He smiled now. "I think you overestimate my influence. But I like the idea. This park would be a perfect place for my own children to ride their bikes and skateboards. Let me talk to some people. Give me your telephone number, and I'll let you know what develops. Oh, by the way, who are you?"

Orion smiled sheepishly. Where were her manners! In her nervousness and haste to get the whole story out, she had completely forgotten introductions.

"I'm Orion. He's Cas, and he's Paul." In turn, they each shook Mr. Capella's hand.

"Well, partners," Mr. Capella said, "good luck. I'll be in touch."

Outside the bank, Paul and Cas clapped Orion on the back.

"Way to go, Orion!" Cas said.

"You're a real politician," Paul added.

Orion beamed.

CHAPTER 15 DETAILS, DETAILS, DETAILS

Orion, Paul and Cas went to the next Milky Way Trail Club meeting with a new plan in mind. "We can set up a booth at the Fourth of July celebration to collect signatures," Cas said.

"The next council meeting is just two days after the Fourth, so we have more than a month to prepare a funding estimate," Orion assured them. "Mr. Capella, the Pentagon National Bank President, has agreed to take our plans and work with Major Ursa and Ms. Cassio to prepare all the paperwork we need."

But they had so much to consider, so much to do. When would the fun begin, when they were grown-ups?

The Milky Way Trail Club worked furiously to prepare the petition and funding estimate before the Fourth of July. Orion's parents helped her print the signs and petitions on the computer, and the twins' parents helped by seeing that they met all the festival requirements to set up a booth to collect signatures.

Major Ursa, Ms. Cassio and Mr. Capella were made honorary members of the Milky Way Trail Club, and they asked the club's opinion on every funding detail.

But it seemed as if each detail meant coming up with yet another plan. How much would it cost to clear the trail? How much to pave the trail? If there was crime in the area, would they have to provide money for security?

To find out the cost to clear the trail, the Milky Way Trail Club had to walk the whole trail and tag each tree less than four inches in diameter for removal. They also had to check for endangered species, plant and animal, that might exist along the six-mile stretch.

Luckily, none seemed to live along the railroad bed, though they found a family of red cockaded woodpeckers in a group of old long leaf pine trees, a gopher tortoise that had a great den in a small cliff of sand along the trail, and a patch of pitcher plants along a swampy area. These areas would have to be fenced off, which would increase the cost.

Paving a trail in the Florida Panhandle entailed making a sandy path secure enough to keep it from eroding out from under the pavement. Fortunately, the railroad bed was still intact, except for a segment that had been torn up by logging trucks when the area had been clear-cut and a long-leaf pine forest had been planted. Mr. Capella persuaded the Scorpion Paper Company to donate time and equipment. Since the paper company had planted the pine forest, they were anxious to see the area appreciated and gladly agreed to pave the trail.

Was there crime in the area? Paul thought of this one, but Orion hadn't even considered it. The club had an anxious wait while Major Ursa and Ms. Cassio looked into old records, checking for any crimes that might affect whether or not their path received approval. They discovered that the only crime ever committed along that six-mile stretch was a real train robbery in 1939. A payroll shipment on its way to a logging company was robbed by a bandit dressed in a long black riding coat, large-brim black hat and a red bandanna tied over his mouth. Since the train robber had never been caught, the kids kept the wanted poster close at hand, just in case he ever came back to the scene of the crime. According to Ms. Cassio, he would only be around a hundred years old by now, so they wouldn't have any trouble catching him.

But all of the days spent working to answer these questions made the kids impatient.

"Orion," called Paul and Cas through her open bedroom window, "come on out and play!"

Orion got up from her desk and went to the window. The twins stood below, skateboards at the ready.

"Give me a couple of hours to finish working out these figures," she said. "Then I'll be down."

"Orion, we haven't had time to ride our boards since before spring break," the twins protested. "All you ever do is plan, plan, plan. You're still a kid, or have you forgotten?"

Orion looked down at them and wondered if it really was worth all the hassle. They were right, all work and no play makes you no fun to be around. She felt as if she lived for this trail, and no one else could equal her dedication to the project.

Orion considered going out to play, but she said, "After the Fourth of July celebration next week it will all be in the hands of the town council. All they need is the petition and the funding estimate, and we'll be ready to build our Milky Way Trail."

Her words didn't sound convincing even to her, but she knew that, if they worded the petition right and prepared a sensible estimate, the town *would* support them; they just had to get the signatures. Mr. Capella's proposal was quite reasonable according to her parents, and there were more than 30 kids ready to pass out pamphlets while their parents and sponsors collected the necessary registered voters' signatures.

"It will all be over soon, and we'll have our skate park before the school year begins," she said reassuringly.

Canis Major, the Big Dog

As the cold winter arrives, Canis Major, Orion and Taurus, the winter hunting group, span the night sky from east to west. Orion, in the center, battles Taurus, with his trusty dog, Canis Major, at his feet.

Canis Major rises in late summer following Orion the Hunter. Find the Big Dog by using Orion's belt as an arrow pointing toward the southeast at Sirius, the brightest star in the northern hemisphere. On cool fall mornings, the collar-star dominates the eastern pre-dawn sky. Sirius is so bright because it is only eight light years away from us. This means that, if we could travel at the speed of light, it would take us eight years to arrive there.

Canis Major
and the Dog Star
Sirius

Chapter 16 The Milky Way

Once the town council gave final approval, the community worked feverishly to finish the trail before the school year began. Orion and the Milky Way Trail Club watched in amazement as parents, neighbors and businesses arrived to help make the old platform into a real skate park. The Scorpion Paper Company cleared and paved the trail, while Mr. Capella himself installed guard rails on the upper platform. By mid-August, the trail and skate park were finished.

The town council had planned a huge celebration for the new park's grand opening, and finally the day had arrived. Orion and her mom and dad were loading the car with picnic supplies and gallons of water as the sun crested the horizon.

"Are you ready for today, Orion?" Mom asked as they drove the short distance to the head of the trail.

Orion couldn't talk she was so excited. She had hardly ridden her board that entire summer.

Orion glanced down at the brand new skateboard in her lap. She had walked dozens of dogs, mowed a hundred lawns, and washed a thousand cars to earn the money for this treasure. Orion looked down at her sash and checked out the high-tops with the blue-sparking heels; she tapped her knee pads together, adjusted her elbow pads and sighed. Yes, she was ready!

Her heart leaped when she saw the streamers and "Grand Opening" sign over the finished arena. A thick, bright red ribbon stretched across the upper platform ramp. New painted lines; picnic tables; the shiny guard rail. The smell of fresh-cut wood filled the air and made her dizzy with delight. As they pulled into the parking area, she unfastened her seat belt, grabbed her board and sat poised by the door handle waiting for the engine to stop. She was the first! No one else was there. King of the hill!

Silence. She leaped.

Two steps from the car to the sidewalk, one fluid motion and she was soaring on her board. Ramps, walkways, the pike, she took it all in. She soared down the eastern ramp and flew up the western pike. When she was in midair, she pulled her knees up to her chest, turned the board back toward the sun and stretched the entire length of her body down to meet the pike wall.

The sun caught the crystals on her belt and hat. Light shot out in every direction as the golden beams of the sun separated into rainbows like light through a prism. The red stones on her shoulders glittered like rubies, and the blue sparks on her heels flashed like lightning when she made contact with the wall. Her head, her stomach, her feet and her heart tingled with excitement as she flew down the ramp. What a feeling!

Orion lifted her right foot just enough to raise the front of the board off the ground, turned in the center of the arena and came to a halt. Still facing the sun, she turned slowly around and took in the whole scene once again, but this time she wanted to imprint in her mind every detail, every shadow and ray of light, every smell and, most of all, every feeling she felt right now. This must be what it's like to win the Olympics, she thought looking around the magnificent new skate park.

The center where she stood had a ramp at every side. The pike was built along the upper platform. A long sloping ramp ran from the upper platform to the lower platform, and a hairpin turn with a 45-degree slope led to the center where she stood. It was truly a dream come true. *Her* dream.

"Earth to Orion, come in, Orion!" The silence was broken as Paul and Cas flew over the ramp. They looked so impressive! They came to a board-scraping halt and gave Orion a double high-five. She asked if they wanted to learn a new routine she had been imagining. They set right to work practicing the intense slides and maneuvers, while their parents prepared for the day's festivities.

By the time Major Ursa and Ms. Cassio arrived, the whole Milky Way Trail Club was assembled, each with their own opening routine to perform. Mayor North gave a speech that seemed to last forever, and finally it came time to cut the ribbon.

Orion had her board in hand, ready to fly down the nearest ramp as soon as the ribbon dropped to the ground, when she heard her name over the public address system. The mayor was calling her up to the podium! Orion stepped forward, and Mayor North handed her the scissors saying:

"We are here today to dedicate this bike trail and skate park because of this girl's vision. She saw a need in our town, a need for a place where our children could ride their bikes and skateboards without fear of motorized traffic." The mayor paused and stared into the crowd for a moment.

"But she didn't stop there," she went on. "She not only saw the need, she also inspired her family, her friends, her teachers—and the entire town—to help make her vision a reality. This park exists today, Orion, because of your dedication, because of your refusal to give up when facing the hard work required to make a dream come true.

"The town council has decided to name this park to commemorate what inspired your vision. You deserve the honor of cutting the ribbon to officially open the Milky Way Trail and Skate Park!"

Blushing with pride, Orion snipped the ribbon. The crowd clapped and cheered, and the Milky Way Trail Club thronged around her, patting her on the back and giving her high-fives.

"The skate park is open, let's go!" she finally managed to yell and erupted from their midst. Down the steep pike she flew, her sash whipping behind her in the wind, the glitter sparkling in the hot sun.

The twins leaped down the eastern ramp and met her in the center; they locked arms, spun around with Orion as the hub and then released their spin, sending the twins off in opposite directions to the north and south ramps while she catapulted up the western pike, performed a perfect Ollie and shot back down the wall. The crowd on the upper platform gasped and stepped backward as she whipped over the upper wall of the pike and turned her board. Down she flew through the center, just missing the twins as they crossed, up over the eastern ramp to the parking lot. She pushed the end of the board down, turned around and halted, flipping the board into her arms in the same move.

The crowd cheered. The Milky Way Trail and Skate Park was officially open to the public.

All day she watched with pride and wonder as the kids soared up and down the ramps and around and around the skate park. Everyone in town seemed to be there at one time or another.

Tables and booths were set up along the perimeter of the arena, all gaily decorated and busy with their individual functions. There were free helmets, courtesy of the sporting goods store, for any child under the age of 16 who showed up. Since the helmets were simple, white and functional, a craft table with fluorescent covers, reflective stickers and all kinds of decorations was the center of everyone's attention, especially during the hottest parts of the day.

Everything was so bright and colorful. The local radio station was there broadcasting, the snow-cone man was there, and the bike shop was giving repair classes and renting wheels—all kinds of wheels: in-line skates, skateboards, off-road bikes, BMX bikes, racing bikes, tandem bikes, and even baby wagons that attached to bikes. People coming and going, and coming back again all day long.

By the end of the day, Orion was so exhilarated she couldn't believe it was over. Electricity pumped through her veins as she continued to ride her board. "Just one more time, Mom," she pleaded as she went for yet another go-round. When she finally came in for a landing and stepped off her board for the last time that wonderful day, her feet felt like soft rubber and the solid ground felt like waves beneath her.

Orion had become accustomed to the constant level of noise throughout the day, and the silence of the late summer sunset filled her as the feeling in her legs returned to normal. She looked around; they were the only ones left, and Orion hadn't even noticed anyone leave. The sun lowered itself onto the platform, radiating brilliant red and orange rays of light through the pine forest beyond. Orion stood there without a word and watched the most important day of her life come to a close.

Orion looked up at the now dark sky and said, "Look, Mom, the Milky Way is so bright tonight, it looks like a giant fluorescent trail."

Mom looked up and was so impressed by the stars she said, "Let's stay out here tonight, Orion. It's a perfect night, the breeze is keeping the bugs away, and the Perseids meteor shower should make this a night to remember."

As if on cue, a meteor flashed across the sky, and Orion remembered the meteor that flashed across the sky last spring, inspiring this trail. It seemed like yesterday, but Orion was astounded by how much they had accomplished.

They drove home and packed up a few supplies, then returned to the skate park. When the car pulled into the parking lot, Ms. Cassio and Major Ursa were already on the platform, looking at the stars.

"It's too perfect a night to be inside," Ms. Cassio said. "Orion, you don't know how much this trail means to me. Now, I have somewhere I can go and enjoy being outside."

"I've been riding the trail all day, Orion," Major Ursa said. "I don't think I've ever seen so many people riding bikes in this town. I have a feeling we're all going to be safer because of you."

Orion could feel her face redden. "I never would have worked so hard if you two hadn't encouraged me," she said honestly.

"But it was your inspiration and determination that created this park, Orion," Ms. Cassio pointed out. "You set a good example for all of the kids in this town, and I'm very proud of you."

Orion bent over and hugged her teacher. "Thank you," she whispered. She couldn't remember ever feeling so wonderful.

Orion and her mom stretched out on ground cloths and sleeping bags and watched the stars and Perseid meteors for hours. Orion couldn't stay awake all night as she had hoped; she was so tired from the day's events, and every time a meteor flashed across the sky, she felt as if she were on her board again flying down and around the ramps. She actually felt the sensation of the exhilarating motion, from her toes, through her stomach and up into her heart and mind. "What a feeling!" was the last thought that flashed through her mind before she fell asleep under the summer stars.

When the chill of the early morning woke her, Orion lay in her sleeping bag disoriented for a moment until she saw a meteor streak toward the eastern sky. She turned in time to see the trail it left shimmer and fade away, leaving three shining stars in a row. She closed her eyes, and when she opened them, she saw the giant illustration that had inspired her from the first.

The constellations were all there during the school year, rising in the east early on late summer mornings, traveling high in the sky throughout the winter months and setting in the west before summer vacation.

Toward the north was Cassiopeia, the queen on her throne, and Ursa Major, the Great Bear. To Orion they would always be Ms. Cassio and Major Ursa, her mentors showing her the right direction to go.

Taurus and the Pleiades were no longer vehicles threatening the friends, for they were on their own side of the sky with Auriga, the five-sided constellation Orion saw as the Pentagon National Bank.

The colorful bright star Capella in Auriga actually seemed to be winking its approval at her.

And there were her friends, the twins Paul and Cas, the starry stick figures that make up the Gemini Twins.

But most impressive of all, the constellation that seemed to point out all of these great constellations: the red giant, Betelgeuse, at the right shoulder, the blue giant, Rigel, at the left foot and the elusive sash with the Orion Nebula, hanging below the belt of *Orion the Skateboard Kid.*

The Milky Way

Every star you see when you look up in the sky is part of our own home galaxy, the Milky Way. Our star, the Sun, and its solar system are in the outer edge of our disk-shaped galaxy.

During winter nights, the Earth looks through the outer arm of our Milky Way Galaxy, and if you have a clear night, you can see a billion or so stars forming a dim path through Orion.

On early spring mornings, late summer nights and on early fall evenings, when we are facing directly into the center of the Milky Way disk, we see so many zillions of stars that there seems to be a narrow cloud forming a path across the entire night sky.

Star Chart Shows
The Winter View of
The Milky Way

NORTH

CASSIOPEIA

URSA
MINOR

Polaris

Capella
and Kids

URSA
MAJOR

PLEIADES

AURIGA

GEMINI

TAURUS

Castor

Aldebaran

Pollux

ORION

HYADES

EAST

WEST

Betelgeuse

Procyon

Rigel

CANIS
MAJOR

Sirius

SOUTH

Type Style Shows
CONSTELLATION TITLES
CLUSTER TITLES
Star Titles

AUTHORS

Juanita S. Raymond has been an amateur astronomer since 1985, introducing people young and not-so-young to the wonders of the night sky through classroom lectures, planetarium shows, star gazes, and the publication of monthly star charts (see **www. stargazers.org**). She has been a member of the Tallahassee Astronomical Society since 1985, and has served as Education Chair and Vice-President; she has also been a member of the ODYSSEY Science Center (currently known as the Mary Brogan Museum of Art and Science) since 1990, presenting STARLAB (a portable planetarium) shows at schools throughout the Florida Big Bend, as well as monthly presentations at the Science Center. She has studied the mythology of many cultures in order to expand the learning experiences of young people as they study Astronomy.

Leland F. Raymond has been writing and editing professionally since 1983. His publication credits include personality profiles, business profiles, newspaper features, essays and numerous articles on the subjects of writing and editing. He has been a member of the Tallahassee Writers' Association since its inception in 1985 and has served as the editor of *Markings,* the association's monthly newsletter, since April 1994. He has also provided publishing services for this organization's annual poetry and fiction competition chapbooks since 1995.